What Cloud Is My Grandpa In?

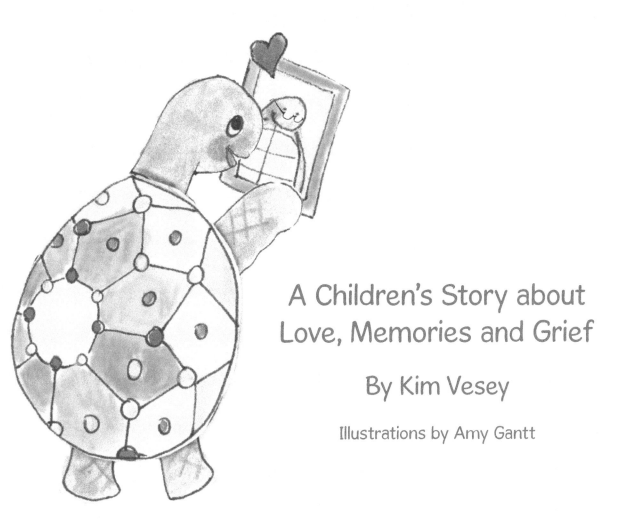

A Children's Story about Love, Memories and Grief

By Kim Vesey

Illustrations by Amy Gantt

WestBow Press books may be ordered through booksellers or by contacting:

WestBow Press
A Division of Thomas Nelson & Zondervan
1663 Liberty Drive
Bloomington, IN 47403
www.westbowpress.com
1 (866) 928-1240

ISBN: 978-1-9736-9373-4 (sc)
ISBN: 978-1-9736-9374-1 (e)

Library of Congress Control Number: 2020910703

Print information available on the last page.

WestBow Press rev. date: 7/1/2020

WESTBOW
P R E S S®
A DIVISION OF THOMAS NELSON
& ZONDERVAN

A portion of the annual proceeds from book sales will be donated to nonprofit organizations which assist grieving children.

Also Available:

What Cloud Is My Mommy In?
What Cloud Is My Daddy In?
What Cloud Is My Grandma In?

Coming Soon:

What Cloud Is My Sister In?
What Cloud Is My Brother In?

This book is lovingly dedicated to my grandfathers, Harvey Lynch and Joe Rocco, who taught me so much about love, humor and dedication to family. I also dedicate this to the loving grandfathers of my children; George Lynch, Ralph Vesey and John Soltis.

Foreword

The death of a family member is painful for everyone it touches. As adults we bring many strengths and resources to bear on this happening, including our experiences with previous losses, our confidence in our ability to survive them, our spiritual practices, and fully developed beliefs about life and how things go.

But small children are different. Their strength in this situation comes not from their here and now experience in the world but from their closeness to the world of imagination, of fairy tales, of the magical and the mystical. Few of us still believe that the world includes magic or that when we speak to flowers or insects or fairies, they hear us. But this is a part of the normal world of childhood. Kim Vesey, in this fourth in a series of six books for children facing a family loss, draws on the inner strengths and world views of young children to offer a sense of closeness, and ongoing connection to those who are very young, and a sense of love that is not diminished by death.

I was seven when my beloved grandfather died. I did not talk about him for a long time. When my mother asked me about this, I had told her that things were different, because now I could take Grandpa to school with me, and I spoke with him for many years.

It is often difficult to talk about death with our children when we ourselves are grieving. It is hard to find the words. Reading *What Cloud Is My Grandpa In?* with our children offers us a simple way to do this and, in the process, find for ourselves the same deep comfort that we offer our children and the realization that love never ends.

Rachel Naomi Remen, MD
Author, Kitchen Table Wisdom
Concord, CA 2020

Acknowledgements

Thank you to the patients I had the privilege of caring for as a hospice nurse. You not only taught me about dying, but you taught me so much about living. I am truly humbled and grateful.

Thank you to the families of the patients I cared for in my career. You allowed me to be witness to the beautiful love you shared, the sacrifices you made to be caregivers, and the pain and grief of saying a final goodbye. You helped prepare me for what was to come.

Thank you to the incredible healthcare workers who cared for my loved ones in such sacred and meaningful ways. That care, as well as your kind care of me, will never be forgotten.

Thank you to the staff of Ohio's Hospice of Dayton for all you have taught me about life, death, grief, survival, kindness, and hope.

I certainly could not have survived the last several years without the love and support of family and friends. My son, parents, sisters, in-laws, co-workers and amazing friends, you have helped to sustain me. Special thanks and sincere love to Patrick Vesey, Tammy and Tim Rowland, Terri Lynch, Joal Baldwin, Lucille Lynch, Jane Soltis, Pam Hunter, Janet Strawn, Julie Murray, and Laura Shindlebower, for your guidance and encouragement to publish this book in order to help others know how to support grieving children.

To Lisa Balster, MA, MBA, LSA, CHA, (director of Care, Patient and Family Support Services and director of Pathways of Hope Grief Counseling Center for Ohio's Hospice of Dayton), thank you for reviewing the book's content to ensure its accuracy and completeness.

Lastly, I am grateful to God. My faith is such a blessing in my life and has been the most significant factor in surviving the profound losses I have experienced. Father Dave Brinkmoeller, will always have my eternal gratitude and love for being a much-needed beacon of hope. I learned through these losses that our loving God is present even in the darkest places.

Introduction

Hi, my name is Kim. I have had the privilege of caring for the dying as a hospice nurse for over thirty-five years. I have watched many families struggle through the grief that comes with the loss of a loved one. One of the most significant struggles is addressing the loss and offering support when there are young children involved.

I have also experienced significant losses in my personal life. My husband, Les, died of cancer in 2006 at the age of forty-nine. My Dad died unexpectedly in 2015. My twenty-nine-year-old daughter, Sarah, died in 2017 from complications of an asthma attack, leaving behind her three-year-old son, Warren. I've chosen to write this book as a way of helping parents and children cope with the loss of a beloved grandfather.

To the parents and those supporting the child/children:

This is a child's story book designed to highlight common experiences related to loss and grief through the eyes of a young turtle, namely:

- There are numerous people in the child's life that can – and – do offer him or her support and care (parents, surviving grandparents, teachers, aunts, uncles, etc.). It's okay to lean on them.
- Grief is like a roller coaster. Some days are sad and hard. There are other days filled with laughter and joy. All these feelings are okay and normal. The challenge is the unpredictability of the ups and downs.
- Each page has a theme which can be used to start a discussion with the child as appropriate. For example, on page eight, you might ask, "what did you have fun doing with your Grandpa?" Or on page 11, you could ask, "what do you do when you feel sad?"
- If the child seems to struggle with reading page after page in the book, consider offering him or her the distraction of looking for some items, which can be found on nearly every page in the story. These include a dog, a brown stuffed puppy, and three characters often associated with loss and grief (a red cardinal, a butterfly and a ladybug).
- Special days can increase the sense of longing for the deceased person. Throughout the book are several simple ideas for working with the child to honor their grief while making tangible remembrances. These are summarized in the back of the book as well.
- It's okay for adults to allow the child to see them grieve. They may need to be reassured that, despite your grief and sadness, you are able and willing to continue to care for them and provide a safe environment. When you share your feelings, it teaches the child that crying and sadness are okay, as are laughing and happiness. In our family, we call tears related to grief and loss *"love tears"*. And love tears are always okay. Naming them love tears

differentiates them from other types of tears. When someone is crying and we ask, "Are you okay?" the person can respond, "I am just having some love tears," and we understand.

It is perfectly okay to read through this book as you would any other book. It may also be helpful to go back to the book for special times (holidays, birthdays, and so on) and discuss ways to honor the child's grandpa on these special dates.

Additionally, if you are having a difficult, grief-filled day or days, you may find you do not want to discuss this with your child. It is important to honor your feelings and grief during this time as well. It is okay to delay discussions about grief for brief periods (days) during times like this. If you find you are avoiding discussing this at all, it would be important to engage the support and help of friends, family and/or professionals to help ensure your child has the support they need to get through this difficult experience. Your child's grief experience at a young age, and the support they receive in processing it, can affect how your child reacts and responds to future grief and loss experiences.

Lastly, in this story, the Grandpa dies following an illness. If the child's Grandpa died unexpectedly or suddenly, consider modifying the story with words like, "Grandpa had an accident and went to the hospital." Or "Grandpa suddenly got very sick and his body wouldn't work right anymore." Explain that it was a different kind of sickness than when we get a cold or flu, so the child isn't fearful if one of you becomes ill. Avoid words and phrases that may cause the child anxiety, such as, "Grandpa went to sleep," as the child might be afraid to fall asleep, or for you to go to sleep. The discussion, and your word choices, will depend on what feels right to you and how the child is reacting to what is being said.

I love my grandpa! We do lots of fun things together.
One of my favorite things is when he comes to
my t-ball games and watches me play ball!

I can hear him shout "you are
the best t-ball player ever!"

My grandpa isn't feeling well today. He had to go to the hospital. Mommy said his body is not working the way it is supposed to.

I left him my stuffed puppy so he wouldn't be scared.

Mommy and Daddy looked sad when they came into my room. They told me that my grandpa died. They said he is now living in heaven with God.

I don't know what that means. My dad explained I won't get to see him or hear his voice anymore. I asked him where heaven was and he said, "in the clouds". I wonder if Grandpa likes living in a cloud.

I miss my grandpa a lot. I feel sad, and sometimes
I cry. I wish I could hug him again, but I can't,
so I hug my favorite stuffed puppy.

It is the same one I let my grandpa use at the hospital.

I was at my grandma's and we were outside looking at the sky and talking about my grandpa. I saw a heart-shaped cloud. Grandma said my grandpa was sending his love to me, and that made me feel happy.

I asked my grandma, "what cloud is my grandpa in?"
Grandma said she didn't know which cloud he is in,
but she knows whatever cloud it is, my grandpa can
always see me and will always be watching over me.

I waved to the
clouds and said,
"Hi Grandpa!"

My grandpa used to like to watch me play in the colorful leaves when they fell from the trees. I miss my grandpa, but on fall days, I still have fun playing in the leaves.

The leaves fell from the tree we planted in grandpa's memory. Our dog had fun playing in them too. I hope Grandpa knows I still love him.

Soon it was time to get ready for Halloween. I got to carve my own pumpkin. I felt happy about that even though Grandpa won't get to see it. My mom and dad took me trick-or-treating. I was a big orange pumpkin this year.

I got lots of candy this year. I wish Grandpa was here to see all my candy; he used to take all the good ones.

My mom cooked our Thanksgiving dinner this year. It was
my grandpa's job to mash the potatoes and carve the
turkey. My dad carved it this year and my uncle let me help
mash the potatoes. The food made my tummy happy.

I wonder if someone
cooked a turkey
in the clouds for
my grandpa.

Soon, Mommy and Daddy got out our
Christmas tree and other decorations.
Looking at all the decorations in
the box made me feel sad again.

My mom put on Christmas music. It made me think about my grandpa making funny faces while my grandma played the piano and sang Christmas songs. I hope he is having a good Christmas in his cloud. Thinking about him makes my heart feel happy.

Other times, I feel sad because I miss my grandpa so much. I wonder if Santa Claus will find my grandpa this year.

Today we got lots of snow. My grandpa used to love helping me build a snowman. I asked my dad to help me today. He tried hard, but my grandpa was the best snowman builder.

Don't worry Grandpa, I will teach Dad how to do it better next time!

On Valentine's Day we made red paper hearts at school. I really wish I could give mine to my grandpa. I decided to put it under my pillow. Happy Valentine's Day, Grandpa. I love you!

On Easter, we went to church and sang songs.

After church we had an Easter egg hunt. Special days seem to make me sad and sometimes they make me cry.

I found the gold egg, and that made me laugh and feel happy. Daddy says it's okay to laugh and be happy, even if my grandpa isn't here anymore.

On the first day of spring, Grandpa always planted his vegetable garden. My grandma said she would help me plant tomatoes this year. Then we can enjoy eating them all summer. Grandpa would be so proud of us.

On Father's Day, I cried. Mommy started crying too and said, "it's ok to cry". We went to the park and played on the playground. Before we left, my daddy brought out a "Happy Father's Day" balloon. They let me write a message to my grandpa on it, and I sent it up to him in his cloud.

One morning my mom told me, "today is Grandpa's birthday." I said, "I hope he is having fun." Do they have birthday parties when someone is in a cloud, I wondered? Mom and Dad said we could make a cake for Grandpa's birthday and sing happy birthday to him. I got to help decorate the cake with lots of sprinkles. When we sang happy birthday to him, I sang extra loud because I wanted to be sure he could hear me.

I also drew a picture of a rainbow and Grandpa and me fishing. Dad asked me to tell them about my picture. Mom wrote things on the back of the picture and told me she would save it for me.

HAPPY BIRTHDAY GRANDPA

When I got into bed, I whispered, "I hope you had a good birthday, Grandpa!"

Sometimes days like today, I have two feelings at once. I am happy that it's my birthday. I am also sad because my grandpa isn't here for my party. I am happy that there are lots of people who love me, and they are here to help me celebrate. I got lots of presents! We had my favorite cake with candles on it. I think my Grandpa would be happy too.

That night, I lay down to go to
sleep, thinking about my party.
My birthday made me smile
and my heart is happy. I told
my grandpa I will always miss
him and love him. I got out of
bed and kissed his picture.

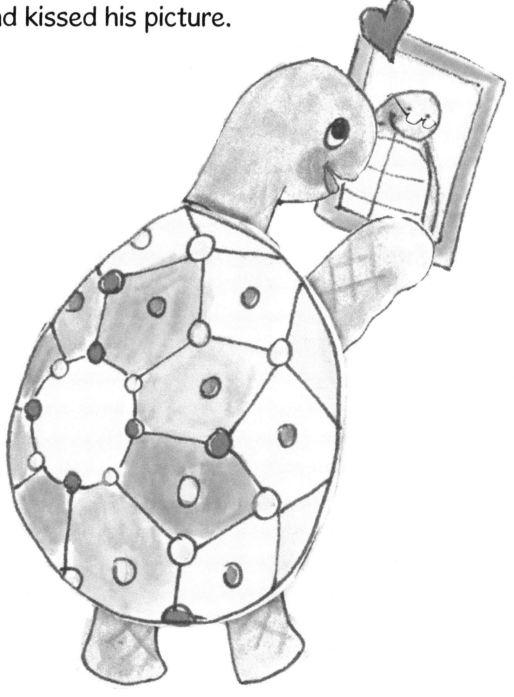

Then I crawled back into bed and covered up with a blanket that has our pictures on it. It feels like Grandpa is hugging me from his cloud.

I prayed, "Thank you God for my grandpa and for taking good care of him."

Additional information and ideas for those supporting and loving the child whose Grandpa has died.

There are numerous ways to help a child process their grief. Just like adults, children grieve in their own way. Among the factors impacting their grief are age, the type of loss (unexpected or expected), relationship to the deceased person, past losses, personality and coping skills. There is no set time frame for grieving as a child or as an adult. It may be helpful to reach out to your local hospice organization, a local children's hospital, your pediatrician, and/or a teacher or school counselor for assistance. Check with these resources if your child is expressing ongoing fears, changes in behaviors, changes in school performance, altered sleeping or eating, anger, deep sadness or any other concerning behaviors.

When you or your child are grieving, this is a time when praying together can be a source of comfort and hope. Pray for specific things such as, "Please let Grandpa know I love him," or "Thank you, God, for taking good care of my Grandpa". Sometimes our prayers can be for us, such as, "Please God, help my heart not to miss Grandpa so much," or "God, please help me to remember the fun times I had with Grandpa." Whatever prayer comes to your mind or heart (or that of the child) is okay.

Here are some things you can do together to aid in grief processing and/or to create tangible remembrances in honor of their Grandpa. Be attentive to the child's response to these activities. If it seems to stress the child, ask if he or she would like to stop the activity. Assure the child that it is okay to stop. While this story focused on getting through important days and holidays, some "anytime activities" are included since grief obviously occurs on normal, regular, everyday kind of days too.

Some "anytime" activities:

- Look through photo albums and reminisce about happier times. Allow the child to ask questions and answer them as best as you can. Avoid providing too much information, in other words, answer questions honestly and gently, staying focused on the specific question

- Watch videos of grandpa and the child, if he or she seems comforted by them or asks to see them. This offers the opportunity to not only see Grandpa, but to hear him too. A caring adult should be present while the child watches the videos. If watching the video prompts tears – which are okay – ask if he or she wants to keep watching or would prefer to stop.

- Continue rituals that were in place prior to Grandpa's death, such as taking walks or singing favorite songs.
- Go to special places where they used to go with Grandpa. This may be the park or playground. It might be the library or a favorite fast-food place. Invite the child to talk about their memories of these places if he or she wants to.
- Have a blanket/pillow made with photos of the child and his or her grandpa. It may include other family as well.
- Consider having a "memory bear" made from one of Grandpa's favorite shirts, soft pajamas or a favorite blanket.
- Have the child pick out two or three favorite pictures with Grandpa and have them put into a picture frame that can be kept in the child's room.
- Plant a tree in memory of Grandpa in the yard. Together, watch it grow and change through the seasons. You can decorate the tree, or the area surrounding it, on special days (pumpkins at Halloween, ornaments or lights for Christmas, plastic eggs for Easter, and so on). Consider planting flowers in a colorful pot painted by the child and place it near the tree. The child can water the flowers and watch them grow.
- Go to an arts and crafts store and purchase a kit to make a memory stone. The child can decorate it, create a handprint with it, and keep it in his or her room or place it outside for all to see.
- Create a new bedtime ritual which incorporates some of what Grandpa did with the child when they were together (read a book, drink hot chocolate, and so on). Add new tasks to the ritual to make it your own.

Here are some ideas for special days:

Father's Day:

- Write a note to your Grandpa and tie it to a balloon or Chinese lantern (with adult supervision at all times)
- Buy a helium balloon that says, "Happy Father's Day". Allow the child to personalize it with markers and send it up to him. To minimize environmental risk, avoid mylar balloons (latex balloons are biodegradable) and keep the string (that the child holds onto) as short as possible.
- Only with adult supervision and as age appropriate, build a small safely contained fire (for example, in a fire pit). Allow the child to write or draw a message or messages to their grandpa on paper. Help them to toss the paper into the fire and watch the smoke carry the message upward to heaven.
- Go to a favorite place for a Father's Day breakfast. Discuss fond memories and consider ordering Grandpa's favorite foods there.
- Cook breakfast together, making Grandpa's favorite foods.
- Create and leave a card, a handprint (of the child) memory garden stone or another memento at his gravesite.

Child's Birthday:

- Acknowledge that this day is and always will be a very special day. Plan how to spend the day together.
- Order a snack basket, flowers or balloons to be delivered to your home, wishing the child a happy birthday. This will help make the day special and remind the child his or her birthday is significant and will be remembered.
- Plan a birthday party (if this is your normal routine) – this is important – it shows the child's birthday will always be honored and celebrated.

Grandpa's Birthday:

- Ask the child if they would like to celebrate Grandpa's birthday in the "usual" way or start a new tradition.
- Place a special picture of Grandpa in a prominent location. Individuals can write a small note of remembrance during this time and place it in a nearby basket for collection. A young child can draw a picture of a fun memory with Grandpa. The child can tell you about the picture, and you can write what is said. These can be kept until the child is older, at which time they can be shared with the child. Having memories of those who knew the child's grandpa may touch them significantly.
- Make him a handmade card. Consider taking the child to the gravesite to leave the card there.
- Lay in the grass, with the child and stare at the beautiful blue sky and white fluffy clouds. Talk about fun things you have done in the past for Grandpa's birthday.
- Have the child make cupcakes for Grandpa, to decorate and share with family and friends.
- Consider singing "Happy Birthday" to Grandpa together.

Holidays:

- Consider discussing past traditions for holidays (Thanksgiving, Christmas, Valentine's Day and Easter). Identify if the child wants to continue any of the "old" traditions. This can be reevaluated annually to determine if there is a desire to bring back any traditions. Here are some ideas:
- Draw a turkey on poster board and have the child write something they are grateful for in each feather. Include a feather with "Grandpa" on it.
- Put a framed picture of Grandpa, and if safe, a candle on or near the dinner table for each holiday. Consider using a battery powered candle if available.
- On Valentine's Day, make a Valentine for Grandpa, and have the child place it under his or her pillow. Or they can take it to the gravesite or put it on the refrigerator for all to see.
- Have an Easter egg hunt on Easter. Special eggs may contain the biggest rewards.
- Share that Grandpa is with Jesus in heaven this Easter. Ask age appropriate questions. For example, "What do you think Jesus and Grandpa are doing to celebrate Easter?" Or "Do you think Grandpa is having an Easter egg hunt today too?"

- For Christmas, assure the child that Santa Claus will come this year (if consistent with your family traditions).
- Read traditional stories and watch Christmas videos. Acknowledge the importance of reminiscing, as well as creating new memories.
- Allow the child to help decorate the Christmas tree and put the angel on the top of the tree.
- Consider making memorial ornament(s) for the tree
- Go caroling in memory of Grandpa
- Make a donation in memory of Grandpa to a local food bank or to help provide gifts for less- fortunate families and children

Follow your heart and pay attention to the child. If it feels right -- even if it results in tears --it is okay. If the child doesn't seem to want to do the activity, then do not force him or her. If you are not comfortable doing the activity, do not do it. There are two important things to remember. First, we all cope in our own ways and according to our own timetable. Secondly, it is essential to ensure the child is aware of being in a safe environment, where you and others will care for him or her, and of your unending love.

My prayer for you is that in this time of immense pain and grief, may this book and these suggestions help bring a closeness between you and your child that neither of you will ever forget. May God blanket all of you with His mercy, hope and love. I truly wish each of you peace.

Kim Vesey

CPSIA information can be obtained
at www.ICGtesting.com
Printed in the USA
BVHW021535150122
626291BV00004B/21